BLACKA

Previous publications by the author:

In flux (out of print)

Godma (2006, Lulu.com)

Dem Seh (2011, Lulu.com).

BLACKA
Storythms
Owen Ifill

ARCHWAY
PUBLISHING

Copyright © 2021 Owen Ifill.

All rights reserved. No part of this book may be used or reproduced by any means, graphic, electronic, or mechanical, including photocopying, recording, taping or by any information storage retrieval system without the written permission of the author except in the case of brief quotations embodied in critical articles and reviews.

This is a work of fiction. All of the characters, names, incidents, organizations, and dialogue in this novel are either the products of the author's imagination or are used fictitiously.

Archway Publishing books may be ordered through booksellers or by contacting:

Archway Publishing
1663 Liberty Drive
Bloomington, IN 47403
www.archwaypublishing.com
844-669-3957

Because of the dynamic nature of the Internet, any web addresses or links contained in this book may have changed since publication and may no longer be valid. The views expressed in this work are solely those of the author and do not necessarily reflect the views of the publisher, and the publisher hereby disclaims any responsibility for them.

Any people depicted in stock imagery provided by Getty Images are models, and such images are being used for illustrative purposes only. Certain stock imagery © Getty Images.

Previous publications by the author are *In flux* (out of print), *Godma* (2006, Lulu.com), and *Dem Seh* (2011, Lulu.com).

ISBN: 978-1-6657-0028-3 (sc)
ISBN: 978-1-6657-0026-9 (hc)
ISBN: 978-1-6657-0027-6 (e)

Library of Congress Control Number: 2020924098

Print information available on the last page.

Archway Publishing rev. date: 02/26/2021

I thank my immediate, extended, world, and galactic families for the privilege of being a member of this collective. I love you all. Special thanks to Paul King, Pauline Baird, and Francis Bailey for taking the time to review and give commentary for the back cover blurb. My gratitude to Albert Rodrigues (Red Spot) for his encouragement and his belief in me, sometimes more than I believed in myself. Everybody needs a Red Spot.

I acknowledge Buxton, and Guyana by extension. You have always been a firmament in my life.

Last but not least, I thank COVID-19 for the time and space it provided for the completion of this book.

Love
is all there is.
Nothing else is true,
however real
it may look
or feel.
One love.

CONTENTS

Blacka 1

Bullfrog 27

Black Duss (Dust) 45

Stray Daag 59

First Lady 77

Bitta Pill (Buxn Fly Trap) 105

Blackmaan-Khulli 123

Glossary 139

BLACKA

The day
I went looking for Blacka
was hot,
really hot.
It was August,
and it was one
of those Augusts
when the son took vacation,
and the father was holding court.
And he dih vex,
real bex!
It was one of those Augusts
when no rain fell,
and it felt like hell,
day and night.
There were days
that August
when you could lose
a pound
or two
in sweat,
and yet
the weatherman was saying
you ain't seen nothing yet.
There was a heat
in the street,
and it seemed almost

to have a beat
of its own.
It was a time
when wearing a rubba dinky
wasn't a good idea.
Your shoe
could turn to glue
and molten fire.
It was that dire.

Blacka was my grandfather,
and he lived
at Buxton
on the east coast.
At the time,
when I went looking for him,
I was maybe fourteen,
and I had never met him.
All I knew of him
was that he was black,
very black,
unusually black—
black like my father
and me,
only blacker.
He was
my father's father.
I had heard a lot about Blacka,
and about Buxton
by extension,
but I had never gone there.
And I had never met him.

BLACKA

My father
had taken care
to never take us there.
He had left Buxton
in the sixties
as I understand it,
and he had never
gone back.
There were obviously
some major issues
between my father
and grandfather,
because my father
never spoke about him
and never had anything good
to say about Buxton.
On occasions
when I tried
to question him about Blacka,
I would get that look.
And that's all it took
to shut me up.
That look
meant assault
and battery
if you weren't careful.
Back in those days
you could get the shit
beaten out of you
for asking
the wrong question.
Those days

weren't fun,
but that's
just how it was.

I always suspected
that the reason
for the rift
was blackness.
I guess
this sounds inane,
but let me explain.
My father
hated his blackness,
you see,
and hence
hated himself
and me.
I guess
he felt
that Blacka
was responsible
for his blackness,
and so
he resented him.
Blacka was the root
of the tree
that was the source
of his misery.
Anything black
made him angry.
It was
a profound tragedy.

BLACKA

My sister
and brother
had the complexion
of our mother,
who was
"high yella."
That made
for a fierce contrast,
my father and mother
when they were together.
He was a lawyer,
and a successful one,
but his success hinged
on intimidation.
For
he was tall,
he was big,
and
he was black.
And he had a baritone
that rattled chairs
and prosecutors
in courtrooms.
He was
always angry
because his blackness
was always with him.
It, in fact,
was him.
It consumed him.
And in court,
his articulated anger,

his presence,
and his voice
came over
as passion,
power,
and poise.
His cases
were
high drama,
panorama,
melodrama.
He had performances
that would make Denzel
and Morgan Freeman
take notes,
carry coats.
He was that good.
And people loved him.
But he could never
find it in himself
to love himself.

They called him black mamba—
my father,
I mean—
and to say
that that infuriated him
is an understatement.
I guess
it showed how deep
this black resentment
thing went.

BLACKA

I remember
watching my father
chasing after a rasta
for calling him
black mamba.
And that
isn't even the joke,
for he was
on his way to work,
all fly
with suit and tie.
And I won't lie—
I laughed
until I had to cry,
for he fell in the street.
I think
he even lost
a couple of teeth
chasing that guy.
And I kept asking myself,
Why?
But he was okay,
I guess,
except for a missing tooth
and a dirty suit.
But I must say,
that incident
made my day.

I was the youngest,
and I was
largely ignored

in my family.
My blackness,
coupled
with my acting out,
caused it
or was a result of it.
I'm not sure
which was which.
What I know
is that
I was into
all manner of mischief.
You name it,
I was in it
and got away
with it.
I was like
the blow pickney,
the family secret
that everybody knew
except me.
And I loved it.
I got into gambling
pretty early,
for I was good
at math and numbers.
It was easy
to take people's money.
I stayed out late,
skipped school,
and didn't go to church
on Sunday

BLACKA

with the family.
My siblings
hated me,
for they had to be
who my parents
wanted them to be,
prim and prissy.
Part of it,
though,
was straight jealousy.
They wished
that they could be
like me,
black and free.
But minus the black legacy,
obviously.

From as far back
as I can remember,
I was intrigued
by Blacka
and by Buxton.
There were
some strange
and major contradictions there.
I had heard,
for example,
that Buxton was a place
populated by thieves,
murderers, and *nars*,
a place of feuds
and wars.

A place devoid of light,
the kind of place
you had to avoid
at night,
sort of like a cemetery.
A place
you didn't go,
a straight-up no-no.
I heard
that parties ended up
in shootings
and stabbings
over inconsequential things,
like strangers daring to dance
with women
from the village.
I mean,
that's it.
Real intimidating stuff.
And to add to that,
you had men
with false names like
World War,
War Tanga,
War Daag,
Jack Palance,
Hulk,
Killa,
Killala,
Monsta,
Death,
and Satan.

BLACKA

Yes, you heard that right.
Satan lived
in Buxton.

But then
I also heard
of another Buxton.
A place
of community
and caring.
A place
of resistance and daring.
A place
that valued education,
culture,
and its history.
A strange contradiction,
a perennial mystery.
And my young mind
could not bridge
these contradictions.
I could not reconcile them.
They did not meet.
They could not meet.
The tendency of most
is to reject one
and to accept the other,
for it makes things simple.
It gives
peace of mind.
You no longer
have to go through

the mental gymnastics
of trying to make sense
of that which seems
to make none,
to finish
what obviously isn't done.
But for some reason
I couldn't do that.
I refused
to throw one out
and embrace the other,
to throw out the baby
and keep the bathwater.
I held both concepts
in my head
and watched them
battle each other.
And I guess
it was that pulling
and tugging,
that strange war
that created the intrigue
of Buxton
and Blacka
in me.
I wanted to know
at some deep level
whether one,
the other,
both,
or neither of the stories
was true

BLACKA

and why.
I had no idea
why this was so important to me,
but it was.
It just was
what it was.

I'm not sure
how I got to Buxton.
I was just there.
To begin with,
I didn't decide that day
that I was going there.
I was passing
the East Coast car park
when something
just literally possessed me.
It was as though
I was abducted
by some unseen force
and guided into
and seated
in a minibus.
That was it.
To this day
I couldn't tell you what happened
from the time
I entered the minibus
to when I arrived
in Buxton.
I didn't feel
the sea breeze

that assaults your senses.
I didn't hear
any of the loud dancehall music
that I know
was blaring in the vehicle.
I didn't see anybody
or anything
from the time I left Georgetown
until I arrived.
And I was terrified.
I wasn't sure
what to do
or where to go.
I just didn't know.
I was just
standing there
on the thoroughfare,
wondering if
I should just get back
on the next bus home.
Problem was,
I didn't have a return fare.

Eventually, I started walking.
I knew
that Blacka lived
somewhere down at the back
of the village.
That was as much
as I knew.
Beyond that,
I didn't have a clue.

BLACKA

When I arrived
at the railway line
I wasn't sure
how to proceed.
My head
was on a spin cycle
when I saw them,
a group of men
sitting on a log, *gyaafin*.
They had no horns,
guns, or knives,
at least
that I could see.
They looked
like regular people to me,
so I walked nervously
over
and asked
about Blacka.
They told me
to keep walking
until I got
to the last house.
I couldn't miss it,
they said.
It was kinda *kanwa*.
It looked
like the flag of Guyana.
Blacka lived,
they said,
about half a mile further on,
into the back dam.

And it was hot,
really hot.
Nothing moved
except for an occasional
rice-eater daag
that barked
from the safety of its yard.
The coconut trees
stood stock-still,
and there was this shimmering haze
in the distance.
And there was no breeze.
I walked
until I got
to the bottom of the village,
and I paused,
and then
this feeling
of foreboding
started to take hold
of me.
By now
I was sweating
down to my shorts,
and I was beginning to conclude
that this
might not be a good idea
after all.
It seemed
I had hit
the proverbial wall.
But for some reason,

BLACKA

I kept walking,
and with each step
I was becoming more
and more apprehensive.
And then
I heard it.

It was a drumming.
A strange
kind of drumming.
It was
a kind of drumming
the likes of which
I had never heard.
I knew
I had never heard
anything like it,
and yet
it was eerily familiar.
It was
as foreign as Mars,
yet as familiar
as my face.
And it was disorienting.
And within this state
of disorientation,
I froze.
I couldn't move.
I was suspended
in its subtle groove.
There was
a fast and slow

to it.
An ebb and flow
to it.
A come and go
to it.
A yes and no
to it.
A to and fro
to it.
A high and low
to it.
And it was
sort of suffocating.
It was in
and around me
like a fish
in the sea.
I could feel it
in my toes,
in my nose,
in my hair,
in my clothes.
It throbbed
and bobbed
with this questioning rhythm.
And within this movement
a tension
was created.
And this tension
created a space,
a vacuous space,
and that space

BLACKA

was occupied by a silence,
a throbbing silence.
A silence
that was pregnant
with something,
an eerily familiar something.
It was a waiting silence.
A frightening silence.
And I knew that silence.
I recognized
that silence.

I stood rooted to that spot
for what seemed
like an eternity
but couldn't have been
more than ten minutes.
And then it stopped—
the drumming, I mean.
I kept walking,
by now
not seeing any houses
or people.
I was about
to turn back
when I saw
this rickety bridge
over the trench.
I was standing there
contemplating it
when I saw him.
I immediately knew

that it was him.
He was
the blackest human
I had ever seen,
at that point
or since.
It made you wince.
He was blacker
than Blacks,
Black fowl,
Blackie,
Black an shine,
Nugget,
Bun up
and Tar maan
combined.
And this
is from somebody
who is pretty black himself.
He was black,
a bold black.
A black
that seemed
blacker than black,
or at least
was as black
as black could ever be.
It was a black
that was loud,
that was proud,
that was
otherworldly endowed.

BLACKA

It was a black
that shouted
across the space
that separated us
and laughed
at the light
that burnished him.
A black
with a strange hue,
a weird sheen,
a black
like I had never seen.
A black
that seemed obscene
and would have been
but for
its luster and sheen.
It was an "ohmigaad!" black.
A black
that was an exclamation.
A black
without explanation.
A shocking black!
A statement
of fact.
A black attack!
It locked your eyes
in a sort
of perceptual vice
and left you speechless.
I was in awe.
It was all I saw.

Then he spoke,
and the spell broke.

He spoke,
but I never heard
what it was that he said.
He was huge.
Six-foot-plus
and big to match.
He reminded me of Cano
or Big Black Boykin
from *Fantasy Factory*,
but without the belly.
He had to be
in his seventies
but he looked fifty,
agile and shifty.
He had a huge,
disheveled bongo natty
that fell
every which way
and that had
hints of gray.
It was then
that I saw
that it was him
who had been drumming.
His drum
was beside him,
rustic as can be,
under the mango tree
where he had been sitting.

BLACKA

And he stood there
for a long while,
looking me over
from head to toe.
That is when
I noticed his eyes.
They were huge.
They in fact
couldn't be as huge
as they seemed.
And they were soft,
the softest eyes
that I had ever seen.
Then he smiled,
a smile
that transformed
his face.
A smile
that made him
into a child.
And it took
all of the anxiety
out of me.
And without knowing why,
I felt my face
smile back.
Then he laughed,
a crazy guttural laugh.
A laugh
that shook the mango tree
he was standing under
and that made me wonder

how my father
could hate this man
who was his father.
And without knowing why,
I started
to laugh as well.
We just stood there laughing
like two crazy people.
Then he came
over the bridge,
and he grabbed me,
and he hugged me,
and he touched my nose
and the arch
of my brow.
And then he held me
at arm's length
and looked deep
into me.
I mean that literally.
He looked into me.
His eyes,
his gaze,
seemed to grab my eyes
and fix them.
And he moved his head
from side to side,
all the while
peering intently
into my eyes,
as if searching for something.
I guess

BLACKA

that sounds intrusive
or maybe threatening,
but it really wasn't.
As a matter of fact,
it had
a soothing sort of effect.
I felt
mildly drowsy,
and that was all.
Then he stepped back.
"You have come,"
he said,
and I knew
there and then
that I was home.
I never went back
to my father's house,
and he never came
to look for me.
And I knew
that he knew
where I was.

BULLFROG

I hated school
for more reasons
than one,
but when all
is said
and done,
maybe
my greatest life lesson,
I actually learned
in school.
And by school
I don't mean the classroom.
I didn't learn much there,
beyond
what to think
and how to think it.
And if you thought
that you could question
what you were taught
to think,
think again.
School for me
was a colossal waste
of my time.
The greatest lesson
that I learned,
I actually learned

in the schoolyard.
And what I learned
is that fear
is a lie,
and that,
ultimately,
is why
I left school.

The day
after my birthday,
Blacka called me
into the kitchen.
He was cooking dry food.
He stopped
stirring the pot
and turned to me.
"Wha meck yu nah ah guh ah skool, bhai?"
And I froze.
God knows.
It had been
almost two weeks
since I had last been to school.
And then
he asked the same question,
but this time
in English.
Perfect English.
"Why are you not going to school?"
When elders spoke in Creolese
and then
made the translation

BLACKA

to English,
you paid attention.
In those days
you knew those cues.
That translation
meant bad news.
It meant bellyache,
budshit,
coconut broom,
ole wood
or heavy metal,
and blues.
Down-home country blues.
So I told him.
I told him about Bullfrog.
Bullfrog was the school bully.
Bullfrog was one of those guys
who really and truly
had no interest in school.
That's just how it was.
You know,
he was one of those guys.
He had no books
and no interest
in books.
He didn't even do exams.
Thinking about it,
I didn't even know
if Bullfrog could read.
He was one of those guys
who we called "leff back,"
who hadn't passed

to go to the next class
a couple of times.
He came to school
mainly for sports
and for beatin people up.
Bullfrog was maybe two years older
than the rest of us,
so he was physically bigger.
In addition
he was "Conguh,"
so he was bigger still.
Bullfrog excelled
in track and soccer.
He was strong.
He was fast.
And he was big.
And he was
what we called "hignarant"
back in those days.
Bullfrog looked for a fight
every day;
that was just his way,
I guess.
He seemed
not to be comfortable,
he seemed
not to be able to be,
if he couldn't beat up somebody.
There was an itch
in his brain,
or his ass
maybe,

BLACKA

that he had to scratch
by beatin up somebody.

Anyway,
I heard that Bullfrog
was looking for yours truly,
and in any language
that would mean me.
So I stopped
going to school.
It was that simple.
After all,
self-preservation
is nature's first law.
Bullfrog could eat me raw.
That is all I saw.
I knew
I couldn't handle Bullfrog;
I just wasn't in his league.
The problem started
because I had a fight with Bullfrog's friend.
Bullfrog was out of school,
so he wasn't around at the time.
His friend, Saada Bake,
it seems he felt
that I was a punk
or some "rank mook,"
so he came to test me.
Bullfrog collected taxes.
Yes, we paid rates
and taxes in school.
It was standard operating procedure

back then.
He took a percentage
of your lunch money,
every day.
Bullfrog had to get paid
to defend you
or simply
to not beat you up himself.
I was lucky,
because Blacka would pay me
from time to time
for work I did.
He taught me quite early
to value my labor and time.
How you value your labor and time
is a reflection
of how you value yourself,
he often said.
And when I had no money,
I skipped school
and played gam,
cricket, or soccer all day.
As they say,
you have to know the game
to be able to play.

So Bullfrog was absent,
and his souljah Saada Bake
wanted to run things,
wanted to collect taxes.
So I said no,
not happenin!

BLACKA

That wasn't how
it was gonna go down;
after all,
I was no circus clown.
And he rushed me.
So I beat him
like a snake,
a water snake.
I mean beat down,
real beat down!
Snot and cold
and tears beat down.
Blows like buck bead!
So Saada Bake run home.
And Bullfrog heard
about the happenings
and was looking for me.

Blacka listened
with rapt attention,
but he never once
showed any reaction.
Then he came over
and sat
on the tree stump stool
that he used
to keep the door open.
He went
into a long silence.
Then he said,
"Why didn't you tell me?
What makes you think

you had to deal
with this alone?"
"I didn't think
you could do anything
about Bullfrog," I replied.
That is when he smiled.
That impish smile.
He asked what it was
that prevented me
from going to school,
what it was
that was so powerful
that I was willing
to give up my freedom
because of it.
So I named it.
"Bullfrog."
He said no.
Not true.
Bullfrog
was not the issue.
He said,
if Bullfrog
had another name,
I would be
in the same situation.
Blacka told me
that to solve a problem,
I needed to first face it,
to look squarely at it.
Every "problem," he said,
has another name.

BLACKA

That other name
is opportunity.
It is only
if you face the problem
that you can see the opportunity;
if your back
is to the problem,
if you are running
from the problem,
you can never see
the opportunity.
They have the same face,
you see.

Fear
was the issue here,
he said,
and this
was as good a time as any
for us to look at fear.
"Fear is a lie,"
he began,
"but it is a complex lie.
It is a lie
that has power
because,
like pain,
people run from it.
People avoid it.
People don't engage it.
People don't challenge it.
We do not face it

and advance to it
and poke it
with a finger
to see
that it is
made of smoke.
To see
that in reality
it is really
just a bad joke.
And that
is where its power lies.
That is why
it never dies.
And in addition,
it has many faces,
so it hides
in plain sight.
Hate, for example,
is fear
in disguise.
Jealousy,
anger,
greed,
and arrogance
are fear
wearing different pants.
Fear
is separation.
Fear
is domination,
and fear

is competition.
Fear
is what makes you
only see danger,
what makes you
close your door
to the stranger.
Fear is what hides
and holds secrets,
why we have skeletons
in our closets.
It is why
we do not share
and why we relinquish
our capacity to care.
Fear is the reason,
you see,
for conformity
and orthodoxy.
It does not allow you to be
who you ought to be.
And the truth is
none of this is necessary,
for fear is a trick,
and its value lies
in the challenging of it.
It is a shadow membrane
that surrounds your world.
It is the skin
that holds
your consciousness in place.
Challenging it

stretches it.
Your life
should be about stretching it,
expanding that skin.
If your life
was only
about confronting your fears,
your life
would be a great adventure.

"So yes,
Bullfrog is not the problem
and has never been the problem.
The bully himself
is riddled with fear,
and that
is what he shares.
It is what grants him importance.
Being a bully
is what makes him somebody.
The way I see it,
you have a set of options.
You can hide;
you can stop going to school;
you can forfeit your freedom
to a falsehood.
You can live
in a chicken coop
when the sky is available
and forever wonder
what the sky looks like.
Or you can try

BLACKA

to talk him out of it.
You can use your wit—
you know,
try some funny shit.
If it works,
you learn conciliation,
what to do
when you can't fight
and you can't run.
Or you can fight him.
If you fight him,
you've already won.
You've already beaten fear.
If you win the fight,
it means
you discovered resources
you didn't know you had.
If you lose,
you may get a lesson
in humility,
which you may need.
And you will earn his respect,
along with some lumps
and bumps
and hopefully
no broken bones.
'Jumbie lash'
is obviously always an option,
but it isn't one
that I would endorse.
You have
to make the decision.

Make a decision
and live with it!

"There is a part of you
that essentially
is a guidance system,"
Blacka said.
"If you learn to go there,
to that place,
where
there is no fear,
you will hear
what it is
that needs to be done
or not done."
Blacka had me sit
in his garden
for twenty minutes
every day.
He had me listen
to the coconut branches
as they swayed
in the breeze,
nothing else.
He said
if I asked for an answer
in that state,
it would be revealed,
and I would know it
when I heard it.

BLACKA

I did what he asked
for two weeks
and had practically given up
when one night
I had this dream.
In it,
I watched myself approach Bullfrog,
no fear,
no hesitation.
I was so close,
I could see the whites
of his eyes,
and in those eyes,
I saw fear.
I woke up,
and I somehow knew
that that
was the answer.

I went to school
the next day,
and as soon
as I saw Bullfrog,
I didn't hesitate,
couldn't wait.
I went up to him
and called him out.
We were close,
so I could see in his eyes,
and what I saw
shocked me.
What I saw

wasn't just fear;
it was terror.
I could have pushed him over
with a finger.
Instead
I gave him
a cokenut (head butt),
then another,
then another.
I gave him
an entire trush (bunch).
And he collapsed
right there
in front of me.
And I left
and never went back to school.
My leaving school
had nothing to do with Bullfrog,
if that is your thinking.
The whole incident
triggered a revelation
in me.
I left school
because I learned
a much more important lesson;
I learned
that the system of education
was a system of imposition
and indoctrination;
was based on intimidation,
competition,
and coercion—

BLACKA

on fear,
in other words.
And fear,
as I had discovered,
was a lie.
When I told Blacka
that I was done with school
and why,
he looked to the sky.
And he smiled
that knowing smile.
And that was all.

BLACK DUSS (DUST)

I loved
to observe Blacka.
He was a fascinating study.
He did
many varied things,
but it wasn't so much
what he did
as how he accomplished them.
He made
and sold drums,
and he also taught drumming.
He counseled
and treated people
for various conditions,
and he tended his farm
and flower garden
at the back of the house.
From time to time,
people just stopped by to talk.
One of the great paradoxes
that I noted immediately
was that Blacka
was always busy,
yet he always had time.
He was always engaged
but never hurried.
He seemed to get things done

without any effort—
no stress,
no strain,
no sweat,
no pain.
There was a quality
of ease
to everything he did.
And it so fascinated me
that eventually
I had to ask about it.

One Sunday
after dinner,
we were sitting
in his flower garden
when he started
to play that rhythm.
The one
that he'd been playing
on the day
that I came.
The to-and-fro,
come-and-go
rhythm.
I had almost forgotten it
by then.
And it felt
and sounded
just as mysterious
and strangely familiar
as back then.

BLACKA

That is when
I asked him.
He liked to sit
in his flower garden,
under the jamoon tree after dinner,
to welcome the night.
He smiled,
as I remember it.
He said
that there was really nothing to it.
"All it takes,
you see,
is to give to everything
your totality—
in other words,
to be.
To be present
while doing
whatever you are doing.
When you're eating,
you eat.
When drumming,
you drum.
When shitting,
you shit.
You don't shit
while reading the newspaper
or watching TV.
You don't cook
while thinking
about your cousin in BV.
When you're fully present,

time
becomes your tool.
You use it
as you wish,
for you
are outside of it.
You can bend,
stretch,
or collapse it.
You can do with it
whatever you see fit.
It just takes practice.
I will show you how,
but for now,
there is a story
I want to share with you.

"The rhythm
that I was playing,
I'm sure
that it sounds
strangely familiar
to you,
as if you know it,
as if,
deep in your core,
you've heard it before,
somewhere,
somehow.
But it is vague,
ephemeral,
and nebulous.

BLACKA

That rhythm
is called 'black duss.'
It is your heartbeat.
It is our path,
our way;
it is
in your DNA.
When I was
about twelve years old,
my father taught me that rhythm
on the drum,
and he told a story
to me.
The rhythm was born
out of the story.
It was told to him
by his grandmother,
who heard it from her father,
who got it from his grandfather,
the original Blacka.
The story is 'Black Duss.'
This story
comes down generations
in our family.
It begins
with the reemergence
of black people.

"There was a time,
you see,
when black people
had totally disappeared

from the face of the earth,
the way the Aztecs
and Incas disappeared,
the way
they were razed
and cleared.
There was a black slavery,
you see,
before the slavery
that you have come to know
as slavery,
before the slavery
that you read about
in your books of history.
And when black people disappeared,
when they became extinct,
the collective black consciousness materialized.
It became flesh.
For energy,
you see,
cannot be destroyed.
It changes form.
And it materialized
into a huge dune
of 'black duss' (dust).
That 'black duss'
became the only evidence
of the prior existence
of black people.
And nobody entered those dunes
of black duss.

BLACKA

"And those dunes
became a source
of great fear,
guilt, and superstition,
of anxiety and trepidation.
People could hear
moaning and wailing
in those dunes of black duss
in the quiet of night.
So they built walls
around it,
walls
that towered to the sky,
and they hoped
that black duss would disappear
or die.
And they forgot about it.
And after a few generations,
nobody knew
why those walls were there
or what was beyond them.
They just knew
they couldn't go beyond them.
That was what every parent
told their child,
and they had no answer
when the child asked why.

"Meanwhile,
the society was in constant turmoil.
There were wars and strife,
the gun, the knife.

And a deep anger
permeated life.
There was a deep yearning in all,
but for what
nobody knew,
hadn't a clue.
And over time
this feeling only grew.
Everyone felt
that something was missing,
like sex
without kissing—
for you see,
without black,
white cannot be.
Without black,
white has no meaning,
the way
without night,
day has no meaning.

"And so
there was music,
for example,
but there was no funk
or blues
or jazz
to it.
No drum or bass
to it.
Just flat,
lifeless,

BLACKA

insipid shit.
There was sport,
but there was no athleticism
or passion.
There was style,
but there was no fashion.
And there was humor
and comedy,
but it lacked verve,
all fastball,
no curve.
Even people's laughter
was superficial,
and their dance
was noncommittal.
And the women
had no tense—
an incomplete sentence.
No breast,
no ass,
no curves,
no mass.
And there was a slow suicide happening,
and nobody knew
how to stop it.

"And then one day,
kids being kids,
rambunctious and curious,
one of them
climbed the fence
and went over

into those dunes
of black duss.
And the black nation awoke
and arose,
for it was only love
that could repair
what hate had wrought.
And when that happened,
the world changed.
That which was missing,
the arc
that completed the circle,
was now available.
And the patriarch
of that,
the first generation
of the black reemergence,
was called 'Black Duss.'
That evolved to Blacka.
You are a direct descendant
of the original Blacka,
as am I.
We are a people
who,
like the phoenix,
have risen from the dead.
We will always be here.
The slavery
and segregation
and apartheid
that you have read about
in your history books

are gone.
We are still here.
But with all chronic abuse,
there is always a hangover.
The anger and resentment
of our forefathers
is still very much a part
of the current black psyche.
And current mistreatment
and marginalization
only add to that anger.
The uniqueness
of the black situation
is that black anger
is turned onto itself.
And anger turned onto itself
is hate.
And so
we hate ourselves.
We are killing ourselves
every day
on the streets
of our ghettoes
and barrios
and favelas
and inner cities.
And we have no idea
why we are doing this.

"The angry black man
has become a cultural motif.
We have so believed it,

we have so embraced it,
we have so accepted it
that it has become our creed.
It is what we bleed.
In our interactions
we give it.
In our lives
we live it.
In the lifestyles
of our young people,
they honor it.
They have made a culture of it.
Rap/hip-hop
is a progeny of it,
and jail culture,
addiction, and nihilism
are outgrowths of it.
Its chronic unexpressed manifestations
are given expression
in hypertension,
cancers,
addiction,
diabetes,
and a host
of other chronic diseases.
And the truth is,
it is all a lie.

"Whether through self-hate,
fear,
anger,
victimhood,

BLACKA

nihilism,
or the black consciousness movement,
we live a lie.
We live a lie
because our self-hate,
fear,
and victimhood
are reactions
to a lie.
And the reaction to a lie
is also a lie.
The 'black consciousness movement'
is a lie
because it seeks,
through our cultural stories,
our achievements,
and our history,
to justify our humanity.
To refute a lie.
And the reaction to a lie
is a lie.
These reactions and defenses
are addressing the lie
that says
that we are inferior,
that we are less,
that we are loveless.
That we are the other,
the mother
of misery.
That we are
of some other God

that nobody knows about
or cares about.
But truth,
you see,
needs no defense.
It is
its own defense.
If you don't remember anything
of what I just said,
remember this.
Always remember this.
This is truth.
All beings
are one being.
We are all pieces
of that one being.
You are equal
to any human
who has ever lived
or ever will live.
We come
from the same place,
the same space.
We have one face.
It is the summit
of ignorance
to believe that another
is lesser,
or greater,
than you.
Make that your creed."

STRAY DAAG

I guess Stray Daag
came back to Buxton
for the same reason
that ole folks from America
come back home:
to die.
There is something uncanny
that calls you back
when your back
is against the wall,
when you crash
and you fall.
That calls you back to that place
where it all began,
where the entire village
was your clan.
That place
where you learned
how to fight,
where your imagination
first took flight,
and you believed
that all was possible.
It is actually ironic
that it is the place
where you felt most alive
that you return to

when you are dying.
And he was dying,
or at least
that's how he felt.
When the world you know
is receding,
when you discover
that all the assumptions
you had heretofore believed
and accepted as gospel
are a lie,
it feels like death.
And death
feels like an emptiness,
a dark and dank emptiness.
An unfathomable and eerie emptiness.
A sense
of not knowing what is up
and what
is down,
or if both are neither,
and not caring.
A sense
of nothing mattering,
because there is nothing
left to matter.

I guess Stray Daag came back to Buxton
for the familiarity one seeks
when one is lost,
for a firmament
when all

BLACKA

is turning to smoke and dust.
For the clues
one pursues
when one is seeking meaning,
for the method to the math
that says
that all
is equal to naught.
I guess he came back
because Buxton was home,
because he was born here
and lived fifteen years of his life here,
and the best ones too.
He had "he fuss fat eye an feel heah,"
he "fuss kamaniss an kiss heah."
He swim company trench
wid Big Wood, Gandhi, Planka, an Zap.
Dah is wheh he learn dice an rap
wid Scissors Bread an Map.
He thief coconut,
mango, and gennip,
an ketch fire red an ring neck
wid Keckweer, Wolf, Himpim, an Balla.
He thief fowl an duck
fuh bush cook
wid Snake a Hole, Fiend, Fish, Jumbie, an Took.
And he walked the village daily
from top to bottom.
That was his game.
That was how
he got his name.

He came back to Buxton
because Buxton
was essentially all he had left.
It was the end
of the road.
It was the culmination
of a series of events that,
had they not been so tragic,
would have made a great comedy.
He had been a broker
with Goldman-Sachs
up until the Wall Street meltdown.
He had lived the life.
A life that was a montage
of hedonism and materialism.
The American dream/nightmare.
The women
and the entourage.
The houses
and fancy cars
and cocktails at fancy bars.
The keeping up with the Joneses.
And then it happened;
the unimaginable happened.
Wall Street fell,
and all hell
broke loose.
He lost his job,
and his house was foreclosed
in the mortgage crisis.
Then his wife left,
for the bling was gone;

the sweet was done.
About that
he didn't really make a fuss,
for their life together
was really all about status.
What really bothered him, though,
was that she burned the house
to the ground
before leaving.
And his dog,
the only thing in the world
he could truly say he loved,
died in that fire.
Burned to ash
like yesterday's trash.
That day
was truly hell.
On that day
something in him died as well.

That was the day
that the longing started.
It initially
was just a gnawing feeling inside,
a vague unease.
A sort of allergy,
but without the sneeze.
A nagging ache
that had no localization.
A voice
that had no vocalization.
And what started as an itch

became a pain.
A burning pain.
A forest fire
that was dark
and all-consuming.
And the longing
became a craving.
And he stopped eating
and sleeping.
He lost all interest
in things
that used to be important to him.
And the craving
only grew within,
the way dope fiends
crave heroin.
But he didn't know what it was
that he craved,
and so it could not be satiated.
His whole life
became this thing,
which was essentially
a giant nebulous craving.
But for what
he didn't know.
And all it did
was grow.
There was this huge splinter
in his brain
that he could not reach,
a fortress
that he could not breach.

BLACKA

And then the nightmares began.
They were identical
in structure and content,
and they were recurring every night
in the hour or so
of sleep he got.
He always woke up
struggling, screaming,
and soaked in sweat,
trembling like a leaf
and scared to death.
And he couldn't go back to sleep.
In his dream
he would suddenly find himself
in a deep jungle somewhere,
walking along a long
and winding trail
that led
to God knows where.
And it was pitch-black.
And for some reason,
he could not look to the sides
or look back.
It was a one-way track.
And something
or someone was following him,
was stalking him.
He couldn't see
or hear anything;
he just felt it.
He just knew it.
And he couldn't stop

or retreat.
He had no control of his feet.
Something propelled him forward,
to a clearing
to which he inevitably arrived.
And it was dark
for it was deep jungle;
and it was quiet,
deathly quiet.
A whispering,
still quietude.
And there were never
the usual nocturnal sounds
of the jungle—
you know,
like crickets and birds
or rustling leaves.
And there was always this feeling
of being watched,
of someone
or something watching
and waiting.
Not saying anything.
Not doing anything.
Just watching
and waiting.
And he would arrive
at the clearing
and would collapse
at a particular spot.
And he would lie there
in a state of paralysis.

BLACKA

If it hadn't been a dream,
he probably
would have shit
and pissed himself
at the same time.
He had no choice.
He had no voice.
And that was when
this feeling would overcome him,
the sense
that this someone
or something
was standing over him.
And he couldn't turn
or move
or look up.
And the terror
and panic
would overtake him,
and he would awaken.

This went on
for about a month,
and he was losing weight,
and his mind was a fog.
He had bloodshot eyes
like a strangled dog.
He once looked in the mirror
and didn't recognize
who he saw.
And he was beginning to fear
that he was losing his mind;

his marbles
were starting to unwind.
And he cried out
in despair
from the pain
he could no longer bear.
It was then
that he had the visitation.
He had a vision,
one that appeared
to be in his mind's eye,
in his imagination,
only yet
it wasn't.
It was there,
as palpable and transparent
as glassware.
It was bright;
it was light.
And it had a charge to it
that made his hair
stand on end.
And he immediately saw
that it was his friend,
his childhood friend "Bittle maan,"
who had died years ago.
He was just there,
suspended in air,
smiling his gap-toothed
signature smile.
He stayed awhile,
just hovering

BLACKA

and smiling.
Nothing was said.
Not even a nod of the head.
Then he was gone.
After he left,
for some strange reason
Stray Daag suddenly remembered a saying
that ole people used to use in Buxton.
"If yuh house bun down,
yuh wife lef yuh,
an yuh daag dead,
ah time fuh see obeah maan."
That is exactly
what had happened to him,
and it all had happened
the same day.
That was when
he booked a flight to Guyana.

The Buxton
that greeted him
wasn't the Buxton he knew.
It was August,
but the children he saw
were few
and far between.
And they looked prim and clean.
Back in the day
during August holiday,
the streets were full.
Company trench was the village pool.
Taaga, gam, cheer saal, ketcha,

hide an seek, skootah, cricket—
you name it.
He would find out
that kids now spent their time
playing video games and texting.
Times had changed.
He walked the village
from top to bottom
like ole times,
looking for someone
who was still around
that he knew,
somebody maybe
from his old crew,
and all the while
trying to find the courage
to ask someone
about a good "obeah maan."
He eventually got lucky.
He met Bildad,
a classmate from back in the day,
but he had to pay.
A half baboon skin,
two servings of roast pork,
plus a raise,
for good measure.
Bildad pointed him to Blacka.
He said Blacka
was the best.

Stray Daag went to see Blacka
the very next day.

BLACKA

It had rained heavily overnight,
so there was mud
and water everywhere.
It was slippery as hell,
and Stray Daag fell
into the trench
while crossing the plank
to enter Blacka's yard.
He had just climbed
onto the dam
when he heard the howling laughter.
It was Blacka.
He needed no introduction.
His blackness said it.
He had the complete kit.
He invited Stray Daag in,
still laughing,
and offered some dry clothes
for him to change,
all the while
looking him over with interest.

When he was comfortable,
Blacka invited him to have a seat,
then he sat
across from him.
"Leh mih guess why yuh come;
yuh house bun dung,
yuh wife lef yuh,
yuh daag dead,
an yuh fall een dih trench
fuh cool yuh head."

Stray Daag's jaw fell
to the creaky floor
in Blacka's house.
He started to speak,
but Blacka continued.
"I know why you're here," he said.
"I was expecting you."
"Is this some kind of a joke?" Stray Daag asked.

"No," Blacka replied.
"My jokes,
unlike your life,
have life
and color
and music.
Your life
has none of the above.
And that,
incidentally,
is why you're here.
Your life
has become colorless and insipid—
no laughter,
no play,
alternating between black
and shades of gray.
Your thirst for life,
which is a characteristic of life,
is gone,
is said
and done.
And when life stops seeking

BLACKA

to renew
and expand itself,
to become more of itself,
it can no longer be itself.
For life is,
in a sense,
what it continually seeks
to discover of itself.
Your life
has become a barren wasteland.
It has no rhythm,
no rhyme,
no beat,
no time.
And it is from within this fog
that you search for meaning.
That is why you are here.
And those dreams,
those terrifying dreams.
Those dreams
whose meaning
you have been yearning to know
and from whose terror
you seek respite and shelter.
That is why
you are here.

"What has happened
in your life,
you may want to call bad luck,
or 'somebaddy duh yuh,'
but none of it

is true.
I know you came here
to see an obeah maan,
to find out 'wha dem put pan yu,'
but that
is not what I do.
You create your reality.
Whatever happens
in your life,
whether you know it or not,
whether or not
you have given it thought,
you have created it.
You are party to it.
You are cause.
You can blame others
or circumstances
or the powers that be
in order to avoid that responsibility,
but in truth,
you are the creator,
you see.
You
are always cause.

"We have all come to earth
with an agenda,
including you and me.
We each
have a gift
to share
with the rest of humanity.

BLACKA

And when we get lost
in the slumber of materialism
and complacency,
of victimhood,
anger,
and jealousy,
when we lose sight
of who we came here to be,
we are shocked
back into reality.
What you have judged
as misfortune or calamity
is your alarm clock
going off.
It is you
saying to you
that enough is enough.
It is you
trying to wake you up.
You have gotten
so lost in your slumber
that you have forgotten
that you set the clock.
Your alarm clock
has become a rock
so as to get your attention.
In the African tradition,
it is said
that God first throws pebbles
at your window;
if that doesn't get your attention,
rocks follow,

and if you are still asleep,
then boulders
come through your window.
Your 'kadjkow,' your boulder,
has landed.
This experience
is a blessing
if you cease to judge it,
if you slow down,
still yourself,
and listen to it.
If you surrender
and just be with it,
it will show you where
you need to go from here.
It is life
redirecting your life.
Bless this experience,
for it got your attention.
What you do with it
is up to you."

FIRST LADY

Blacka never scolded me.
He never raised his voice
or lost his poise.
He never sat me down
and told me
that this
or that
was wrong,
that I shouldn't have done
this or that.
His emphasis
was never on
the what,
or even the why.
He always said
that young people
always do stupid stuff.
It was part of growing up.
While learning
to wash dishes,
you had to break a cup
or two.
Nothing new.
It was part of the process,
a component
of the confusing mess
that was a juvenile,

a semi-adult child.
What was important,
he said,
was to see
that it was stupid
and to learn from it.
To grow
as you come to know.

He never raised his voice,
but you knew
when something was up.
The eyes—
those eyes
said everything.
It was a dramatic thing.
He would pause
in a kind of slow motion,
in the middle
of whatever he was doing,
and he would turn,
and those eyes
would burn
into the reaches of your face.
And you just knew
that he was onto you.
His eyes
would meet mine
with their signature shine,
and my head
would bow involuntarily.
I could never hold his gaze;

BLACKA

there was this haze
that would overcome me.
And there was a feeling
that accompanied it,
a feeling of powerlessness,
almost of awe.
And he had this trick
of giving a joke
at that precise moment.
And Blacka was funny.
He had a ton
of jokes
and the impeccable timing
and theatrics
to go with them.
And when I started to laugh
and raise my head,
he caught my eyes
with his eyes
and locked them.
And I could not
escape his eyes.
And that
was when he spoke.
He never punished me.
He gave me assignments
that at the time
seemed like punishments.
Looking back,
his "punishments"
were actually great lessons.
They amplified my understandings.

They broadened my feelings.
They made me ponder things
I normally wouldn't have given
a second thought.
At the time
I obviously couldn't see it.
It wasn't a perspective I had
from where I used to sit.

When,
for example,
Blacka told me
I had to spend a day
with First Lady,
I got weak in the knees.
I broke out in a cold sweat;
I mean,
I was soaking wet.
And I felt
a kind of profound nausea
rising in me.
A group of friends and I
had stoned First Lady.
We had chased him
through First Lot,
which was a plot
of open land
where old Bushkar lived.
With "kadjkow" like rain,
we'd brought the pain
to First Lady that day.
Blacka apparently

BLACKA

heard about it,
and so spending a day
with First Lady
was what my "punishment"
was going to be.

Now,
First Lady was gay,
gloriously gay,
the kind of gay
that left no room
for misinterpretation,
the kind of gay
that seemed like a confrontation,
a sort of dare
that compelled you
to stop and stare.
That way-out-there
kind of gay,
the kind
that blows up a gaydar,
you know,
the gay measuring device.
An eleven
on a scale of ten.
The gay
of all the gesticulations
and gyrations.
The voice,
the poise,
the hips,
the dips.

He had all dat
and a bag a chips.
That genre of gay
that makes fundamentalist pastors
foam at the mouth
and makes women roll their eyes
and cuss out.
I mean,
in-your-face,
in-your-space gay.
First Lady was loud
and proud.
He stood out
in a crowd.
And don't mash his corn,
for he would tell you
how and why
you were born.
That was who he was.

And Blacka wanted me
to spend a day
with First Lady.
You have to understand
that homophobia
was normal in Buxton.
That was just how it was.
You grew up
hating and ridiculing gays.
Those were the days
when gays were beat up
for fun;

BLACKA

they were on the run,
under the gun,
most of the time.
That was the culture.
That was acceptable behavior.
Spending a day
with First Lady
for me
was suicide.
That was something
I could never live down
in Buxton.
So I told him
I couldn't do it,
and I left.
I spent about a week out there
in the village,
sleeping wherever
night caught me.
In a village,
food is never an issue.
I could stop in
at a friend's house
at lunch or dinnertime,
and his mother
would share whatever they had,
even when things were bad.
And fruits
were always plentiful.
But I missed Blacka.
I missed
that atmosphere

around him;
there was a kind of lightness,
a worry-free
sort of state
that surrounded him,
that you felt
and benefited from in his presence.
I missed that,
and it was only after I left
that it became
so starkly apparent to me.
So
after a week
of going around in circles,
I went back home.

When I got there,
Blacka was in his garden
weeding around his flower beds.
I picked up a cutlass
and started weeding
along with him.
He looked up
and smiled knowingly
and continued his weeding.
When we were finished,
he went inside and called me to dinner,
a dinner
of metagee with fresh fish
and loud coconut milk,
with my favorite breadfruit.
It was as though

BLACKA

he had known I was coming.
I lash (ate)
and then lash back (had seconds),
and then he told me
how I was going to spend my next day.
I was to report
to First Lady's house
at seven in the morning,
and whatever errands he wanted done,
I was to get them done.
If he was going anywhere,
I was to accompany him,
and that meant anywhere.
Whether to the rum shop,
to Georgetown,
or to the market.
I was allowed
to express whatever I felt
without being disrespectful,
but I was expected
to be engaged,
to give him my attention
when he so required.
That was all.

I had no sleep that night.
I heard the leaves
of the coconut trees at the back
rustling in the breeze,
occasionally punctuated by the loud thud
of falling dryees (dry coconuts).
I got up

about five o'clock
and had a bath in "company trench."
That was in the days
when company trench
was company trench.
The water was black
and sweet
and soothing.
After a bath in the company trench,
you felt
like you owned the day;
there was a freshness
and a confidence
that filled you up.
There was a magic
that sparkled in your cup.
There was a popular saying back then,
that you could only be a Buxtonian
after you drank company trench water.
These days
you could get typhoid or cholera
from drinking that water.
When I got back,
Blacka was sitting
on the tree stump out front,
tuning his drum.
He barely raised his head
as I went by.
He just said
that I would be having breakfast
at First Lady's house.

BLACKA

I left for First Lady's house
in a state of trepidation.
I stopped
no less than six times
and even briefly turned back.
At times,
I thought I was going
to have a heart attack.
But I got there.
I did.
I felt like that kid
who had stolen from his parents
and knew they were waiting at home.
I stood outside the gate
while a raging debate
was going on
in my head.
Then I saw him.
He came to the window
and called me in.
I didn't move initially.
I was frozen silly,
in indecision,
and then First Lady laughed.
He had a "baad hooman" laugh,
raucous,
loud, and grating,
and I just stood there waiting,
for what
I wasn't sure.
Then it was
as if a door opened

in my head,
and I walked into the yard
and up the stairs.
I went
into a decently put-together house.
Everything was neat,
clean,
and in its place.
He served a breakfast
of bake and saltfish
with balgo,
and we washed it down
with cold swank.
And I was somehow shocked!
And I couldn't figure out
the reason for my reaction.
And then it dawned on me
that I was shocked
because for the first time,
I had realized that First Lady
was somebody—
a person,
a regular human being.
The kind you have been
and seen.
He wasn't some thing
that crawled out of someplace,
from outer space.
First Lady actually did eat,
sleep, and shit
the way I did.
It was a revelation,

BLACKA

the depth of which
I couldn't begin to stitch together.
Sort of like
the way
we don't believe
that drug addicts are people
like you and me,
until they show up
in our family.
It shook me.

There was no conversation
during breakfast.
It was as though
he had been expecting me,
because he never asked
why I was there.
He just glanced at me occasionally
during pauses
in eating his breakfast.
After that
I did some errands for him,
then I helped him prepare lunch.
After lunch
I had to accompany him
to a meeting at Tipperary Hall.
That for me
was a tall order,
and I started to balk.
I dreaded that walk.
But a strange thing happened.
We walked

from Buxton backdam side
to the public road,
and I did not feel uncomfortable.
It became clear to me
that nobody noticed me.
First Lady
had such a stark
and dominating presence
that I was invisible.
When he stopped
to gossip with women,
he was all they saw.
When boys
were shouting insults
and mimicking his gyrations,
he was all they saw.
His light
was so bright,
it created a deep shadow,
and it was in that shadow
that I stood.
It was all good.
And I was thankful,
very thankful.
On our way
back from the meeting,
he stopped
at Covetuous joint.
At the time
Covetuous had the best roast poke
maybe on the whole east coast,
if not the country.

BLACKA

Cars lined up for that stuff.
You had to get it early,
or that's it!
We went to the back
where it was relatively quiet,
and he ordered a half "Harry Wills"
and a malta for me.
He threw a shot,
added some water,
and threw it down.
He ordered some roast poke,
and while waiting,
he addressed me directly
for the first time.

"I am not going to ask you
why you hate gay people.
I already know the answer
to that question.
It is in our culture
and our religion.
I can't blame you.
You may find this difficult to believe,
but there was a time
when I hated gay people too,
maybe even more than you.
I hated myself;
I hated me.
You may ask,
but how could that be?
You must understand,
you see,

that growing up in a culture
that tells you
that something is wrong with you,
that you are an abomination,
that you are somehow
not human,
that you are less
than what a person should be—
it does something to you.
Sort of like the same way
slaves were both told
and made to feel
that they were not human,
that they
were some semi-human construct
that didn't belong
and yet was here.
It lays you bare,
for you could grow to believe it;
you could actually become infected
by the shit,
and especially
during that adolescent period
of confusion and insanity.
And so,
you see,
even though there was a part of me
that said
that this wasn't true,
that this couldn't be,
it could not match

the strength of the part
that hated me."

He threw another stiff drink
as his order of roast poke arrived,
and he started to eat.
After a while,
he continued.
"I grew up in a household
that was homophobic,
and so
I could not validate what I felt.
I suppressed what I felt.
I was effeminate,
and I preferred the company of girls.
I loved girly things
like dolly house and litty.
I hated cricket and soccer.
And I got countless beatings
from my father for it.
The fact that in school
I was at the top of my class
didn't matter a bit.
He said he would beat the she
out of me.
He wanted me to be a man.
And so
I belittled gays
just like everybody else
while hiding what I felt."

At this point
he paused
and looked in the distance.
He took a drink,
then another.
He seemed to be debating something
in his mind.
He apparently had to find
either the courage
or the confidence
to say what it was
that he wanted to say.
I just sat
and watched the play.
Finally, he cleared his throat
and continued.
"Suicide had entered my mind
from time to time,
but only in a fleeting way,
and it frightened me.
I knew
it was heresy.
But eventually
the conflict in me
became so severe,
so rabid,
that it was impossible to contain.
It took up residence
in my brain.
And a house
divided against itself
cannot stand;

BLACKA

it is a structure
made of sawdust and sand.
And so
at some point
those thoughts took hold.
They became bold.
They became nagging
and persistent,
and eventually
I gave in to them;
I saw it as the only way
to resolve the problem,
to bridge the contradictions.
I decided to take my life.
And once I made the decision,
a strange thing happened.
The misery ended;
a kind of peace
took me over,
and I sat down
and planned it all out
in every detail.

"The day I chose
was a Friday.
I walked to Strathspey
to Saadhu store
and bought a portion of malathion.
Then I set out on my mission.
I put the flattie bottle
in my pocket
and made my way to the seawall

via Brush Dam.
That walk
seemed like it took three hours,
yet it couldn't have been
more than twenty minutes.
There was a kind
of eerie quietude
that accompanied me the entire way.
I saw no one,
and nothing moved.
The sky looked huge
and somehow close enough to touch.
The trees danced
with a kind of rhythm
that I had never noticed,
and the road seemed to come up
to meet my feet.
I smelled the salt in the sea breeze
for the first time in my life,
and it was a smell
that created an excitement in me.
A perverse sort of ecstasy.
On that day,
the last day of my life,
I discovered things,
things that had always been there,
that were always near,
but that I had never taken the time
to notice.
It was a kind of weird discovery.

BLACKA

"When I arrived at the seawall,
the sun was beginning to set,
and I sat
and watched it sink
below the horizon.
It was the apt metaphor
for my situation—
over
and out.
I lay down on the seawall
with the bottle next to me
to kill some time
until it got dark.
The breeze was intoxicating,
and I must have fallen asleep
because when I came to,
it was pitch-black
and deathly quiet.
When I looked around,
I couldn't see much,
but I had this feeling
that someone or something
was out there watching me.
I knew that
with a clear certainty.
I reached for the bottle behind me,
and it slipped over the wall,
and I heard it smash
on the rocks below.
A wave of despair
came over me,

and I sat there
sobbing uncontrollably.

"Then I heard the voice.
At first I thought
it might have been my imagination
or the wind
or rain,
but then
I heard it again.
I heard
distinct words.
And the voice said,
'You have come here,
to this place,
at this time,
to end your life,
to die.
To culminate
a lie.
And why?
Why are you so ashamed
of being you?
What could be more noble
than being true?
There is only one thing
at which there is none better than you,
and that
is being you.
It may seem
like a cruel joke
that the bottle broke,

but there is no such thing
as an accident.
There is no phenomenon
called coincidence.
Those two words
are gift-wrapped bullshit.
All this means
is that your time
is not yet up;
you still have shit
to clean up.
You can choose,
choose
to believe
what others believe
about you,
or you can be you.
If you choose
to continue
to hate yourself,
to judge yourself,
to make yourself wrong
in your own eyes,
you will end up here again.
You will continue
to be the source of your own pain.
And so
you are at a crucial crossroad.
You can choose
to be you;
you can choose
to feel

what you feel
and live what that dictates.
And if there are those
who have a problem
with you being you,
tough luck.
Who gives a fuck?
Live that attitude!
Even if they ostracize
and even kill you.
At least
you won't have done it
for them;
at least
your life will have had meaning,
for you lived
your truth.
So go forth,
and be proud
of who you are.
Shine your light
so that those
hiding in fear in the darkness
might come forth.
There are many young people
out there
who await
your coming.'

"And the voice stopped.
And that was when it occurred to me
that there was something

BLACKA

vaguely familiar about it.
To this day,
I can't figure out what it was,
but I could have sworn
that I knew that voice.
And then this state
overtook me;
this state
of paroxysms,
of sobbing like a baby
and laughing like a madman.
I cannot say
how long it lasted,
but when it stopped,
the sky was becoming light.
The sun
was cresting the horizon.
And I watched it rise
in all its glory
and magnificence.
And its warmth and its light
filled me.
And for the first time in my life,
I felt whole.
And I knew then
that my life could never again
be about playing a role.
I don't remember how I got home that day—
just one of those things, I guess.
And I guess you can say
that that is the day
that I came out of the closet,

but that isn't even right.
I blew up the closet,
so nobody else
could hide in it.
That is the day
I was set free;
that is the day
I became First Lady."

I apologized profusely
to First Lady
after hearing his story.
And the walk home
at the end of that day
was the longest walk
I had made in my life.
There was this pain
that I felt,
under my belt,
deep in my belly,
that threatened
to cut off my breath.
I walked
like a dying man,
doubled over,
and I knew I was crying only
because I saw the tears and snot
raining down
on the ground
in front of me.
When I got home,
Blacka was waiting at the bridge.

BLACKA

He grabbed me,
and he held me
in an embrace
that had no description.
And when I had cried myself out,
he held me
at arm's length
and looked
deep into me,
the way he had looked
deep into me
the day I arrived.
And he said to me
that I had just experienced
but a fraction of the pain
that gays experience every day.
I went straight to bed.
And that is how
First Lady became my friend,
how my reign of terror against gays
came to an end,
and how he profoundly
changed the trajectory
of my life
and me.

BITTA PILL
(BUXN FLY TRAP)

There was this doctor
who once came to see Blacka.
He had come back
on holiday,
from England
or America,
who's to say?
One of those doctors
thoroughly indoctrinated
in the Western way,
one of those guys
who had nothing good to say
about people like Blacka
and what they felt
he represented.
He was annoyed,
or more accurately,
he was livid,
because his mother
came to see Blacka
on the regular,
because she believed in Blacka,
because Blacka
was in fact
her de facto doctor,
and he couldn't convince her otherwise.

She essentially ignored
his expert advice.

I guess
it felt to him
like being rejected
by his mother.
For if she didn't believe
in his exalted profession,
if she didn't believe
in what he had essentially come
to identify himself with,
and as,
then she didn't believe in him.
Maybe his pride
was hurt;
maybe he had issues
of self-worth.
Or maybe
he just really believed
that Blacka was a thief
and a charlatan,
a garden-variety con man
like Romoko and Zoltan.
What is certain
is that the guy
was hot around the collar
when he came to see Blacka.
He went
on a long diatribe
about Blacka exploiting people's superstition
and called him

BLACKA

all different versions
of a con man.
And all
in perfect English.

And Blacka sat
on his tree trunk stool
and listened to him,
consciously,
deliberately,
until the steam stopped
coming out his ears,
until he came
to a state
where
he could hear.
Then Blacka smiled
and responded in a tone
that was both soft
and even.
He told him
that he understood
how he felt
and why he felt
how he felt.
Blacka told him
that there were some issues,
however,
that he thought
that he should ponder,
not the least of which
was how Western medicine

was practiced.
Blacka told him
that if he had taken the time
to ask his mother
why it was
that she came to him
and not her doctor,
he could have saved himself
all this bother.
"Your mother came to me,"
Blacka said,
"because she was frantic,
because her doctor
was making her sick,
literally
and figuratively.
She came to me
because
she had become a pharmacy.
She had pills galore.
And each time she went,
there were more.
She had pills
for her ills,
and then she had pills
to alleviate ills
caused by those pills.
It gave me the chills.
And each time
she went to her doctor,
she felt worse
after seeing him.

BLACKA

For doctors have a practice,
you see,
of telling patients
only what is wrong with them.
That which is normal
or right
is never emphasized.
She would hear,
for example,
that her kidneys
weren't well,
but he never told her
that her heart
was as sound as a bell.
He kept reminding her
of her gallstones
but never commented
on the health of her bones,
for her age.
I guess he assumed
that she would deduce that.
And while that may be fair,
these are things
people need to hear.
It is important
for people to see
that you see them
and not just their disease.
And so
it is no mystery
why people hate

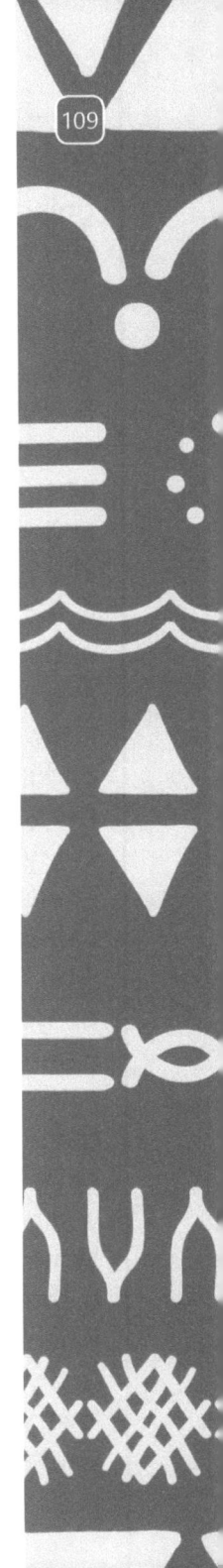

going to the doctor,
you see.

"Doctors have patients,
while I have family.
Everybody knows me
and can speak freely
with
and to me.
The reason for that
is that this is a village,
and in villages
everybody
knows everybody,
and consequently
everybody knows
everybody's business.
That's just how it is.
I already know
who has back pain
or 'goadee'
when they come to see me.
And because they know
that I know
what I know,
what is there to hide?
What in fact
is the value of false pride
when this is public knowledge?
In a village
'everybaddy know
who ah gee blow,

who ah teck blow,
who nah know
dat dem ah get blow,
an who
ah Christmas blow blow.'
Ah suh it go!
I suspect, though,
that the reason for your ire
isn't so much
that your mother is a patient of mine
as it is that
she is now doing fine,
minus painkillers
and benzedrine.
A 'bush doctor'
had the temerity
and the ingenuity
to facilitate the healing
of your mother.

"It is not even her doctor's fault,
I might add,
for he is a product
of the model,
for doctors have been taught
to see patients
and not people.
To see disease and illness
and not people
in various stages
of transitioning to wellness.
And what further complicates the issue

is that Western medicine
does not see
beyond the body
and its parts.
It, in fact,
sees the body
through its parts.
And its structure
mirrors this.
And so
you have specialties
and subspecialties
for each part
and each part's parts.
The tree
keeps branching at the top
while the trunk
keeps getting thinner.
Such a tree
must hit a wall,
has to fall.
And because the body
is seen through its parts,
you treat the parts,
which are essentially the symptoms.
So this complex
and frankly ridiculous ritual
has been developed,
that names
and classifies diseased parts,
when all disease
is actually one disease.

All illness
is one illness.

"All illness,
as all else
you see,
is a factor of vibration.
All is vibration.
That is not debatable.
There is a vibration threshold
that corresponds to health
and below which
is sickness or disease.
Raising vibration
promotes health,
and lowering vibration
promotes or creates disease.
A significant amount
of what is practiced in your medicine
actually lowers vibration.
And outside
of even your approach
and your precepts
is the fact that
some of the medicines you prescribe
lower vibration as well.
It would probably be a stretch
to say
that the medical establishment
created chronic disease.
It would be accurate,
however,

to say that
in partnership
with the pharmaceutical industry,
you have made
a significant contribution
to its creation
and maintenance.
And for this
you have created medicines
that create new diseases
for which
you must find
newer medicines.
That is the trend.
It is a maze without end.

"Health,
as I said,
is about raising frequency,
and that is what I do
for all I see.
My techniques
are actually quite simple.
These are things that
our foreparents practiced
but that have been forgotten
or abandoned.
What I do
is nothing new.
I did not invent
what I do.
It consists,

BLACKA

essentially,
of a cleanse and detox,
light water therapy,
meditation,
and fasting and breath work.
I use herbs
when necessary.
For stress and worry
and problems sleeping,
I teach drumming
as meditation,
and I advise
long barefoot walks
in nature.
Mother Gaia
is a master healer.
Many of the so-called psychiatric illnesses
such as anxiety and depression
are caused
by emotional repression,
by people losing their ability
to process their emotions.
That is why
people become addicts
of any sort,
whether to drugs, sex, work, food,
money, or TV;
they are distracting themselves
from what they feel.
They are afraid
of feeling,
and feeling

is healing.
They can be healed
by walking barefoot
or lying on the ground,
for Mother Earth
is a conduit,
bar none,
for the effective processing
of emotion.
Our children these days
aren't allowed to ground.
They have no relationship
with nature and Mother Earth.
They have tablets
before they can talk,
and they have shoes and slippers
before they can walk.
They don't know
what the earth feels like underfoot,
and you, Doc,
have no idea
of the healing wonders
under your boot.

"And further,
what you don't know
is that half of your so-called diseases
would disappear tomorrow
with the elimination of dairy,
processed foods, and sugar
and the increased intake
of water.

BLACKA

Food allergies and intolerances
abound these days.
It has been shocking
to some of the people I see,
who have been healed
with simple elimination diets,
for conditions
for which
they had been taking meds
for years
with no resolution.
Last
but not least,
I have conversations
with my people,
for that
is who they are.
They are not patients.
I engage them.
Joking,
laughter,
and levity
are an integral part
of my therapy.
They are an important part
of the arsenal
in the raising
of vibration.

"What I do
has been ridiculed,
outlawed,

and forced to the fringes
over the years,
but truth
always triumphs.
Vibrational medicine
will eventually
render Western medicine largely obsolete.
I know
that you are thinking placebo,
for that is the default place
that you guys go.
But even
if that is so,
if it is just pure
and simple placebo,
what of it?
If the patient is better,
what does it matter?
It seems the means
mean
more to you
than the end.
Your way, it seems,
must be
the way,
and damn the results.
Well,
your patients are now
having their say.
And they are saying no
in a big way.
And finally,

BLACKA

I must comment
on what your profession holds aloft
as your gold standard:
the double-blind study,
the jewel
in your armory.
Its name,
incidentally,
is very appropriate,
for it actually is the case
of the blind
leading the blind,
for it has become apparent
to some branches of science
at least,
though mystics
have always known this,
that consciousness is one.
That subject
and object
are not two,
are not
me and you.
So who
is fooling who
while studying who?
Does medicine
even have a clue?
And so
double-blind studies
are actually nonsense
masquerading as science.

The truth
of the matter,
as you will come to know,
is that we are both
using placebo,
but mine
is powered by love,
which has a force-multiplying effect,
as opposed to yours,
which has debilitating side effects.
If medical science were to admit
that objectivity is a myth,
where would that leave it?
What, in fact,
is it?
What would be its merit?

"In essence,
Doc,
what health looks like,
what health actually is,
is a child.
A child
before she was impacted
by the beliefs,
the limits,
the divisions,
the judgments,
and the prejudices
of the society.
That child is health.
She is

high energy
and spontaneity.
She is
laughter and levity.
She is creative,
and she is curious.
She is excitement
and ease
as opposed to torpor
and dis-ease.
She is play.
She lives
in the moment.
She is light.
She is elevated vibration.
She ultimately
is love.
And so
it seems, Doc,
that we have come
to this place,
this weird place,
that says
that love and health
are one and the same.
They are aspects
of the same game,
which is played
in those higher vibrations.
So
what's up, Doc?
What are your thoughts?"

And he never answered.
He was just standing there,
his eyes bugging
and his mouth
wide open,
and he was drooling
from the corner of his mouth.
And the flies
were buzzing in and out
of his mouth.
For a minute,
I thought
that maybe he had had a stroke,
or he was maybe playing
some practical joke.
But he suddenly jerked,
came to himself,
looked around wildly,
and left.
He never came back,
but before he left the country,
dem gee am wan name
"Buxn fly trap."
Nah dah?
Ah dah!

BLACKMAAN-KHULLI

In Buxton
they called him
Blackmaan-khulli (coolie),
for no one knew his name,
or cared
to know it
for that matter.
That wasn't
how Buxton was
or is.
In Buxton,
they christened
and they named you,
and that
was simply that.
And that
was the name
that they gave to him.
He had no say in it.
Almost everybody had a false name
in Buxton.
It was a rite of passage
of sorts,
though some
like Wallababy,
Eshem,
Putch,

and Stiff Shit
never appreciated it.
In fact,
they took
extreme exception to it.
And false names evolve,
for they are alive;
they live
and breathe
in the lives
of the people they represent.
Long names are abbreviated
and truncated
for convenience.
And so his name
became Khulli,
straight Khulli,
the way Shit Koge
became Koge.
He responded
to Koge,
but he only responded
to Shit Koge
if "yu buyin a quarta,"
for then
it was another matter.

They called him Blackmaan-khulli
because he was as much blackmaan
as he was khulli.
He was as much cook-up
and metagee

BLACKA

as he was dhal and rice
and roti and curry.
He lived
in both worlds
and understood
and appreciated both worlds.
He knew Queh-Queh
and Nancy
as well as he knew
Jhandi and Dig Dutty.
He lived seamlessly
in that space,
in
and in between them.
So he had a perspective,
a singular something,
that was as unique
as it was interesting.
He had a window to both worlds;
his feet
were firmly planted
on both properties,
and he had the capacity
to shift as he pleased.
His perspective was singular,
for he had one,
the other,
and a third,
which was a meeting
and melding of both,
which essentially
was neither.

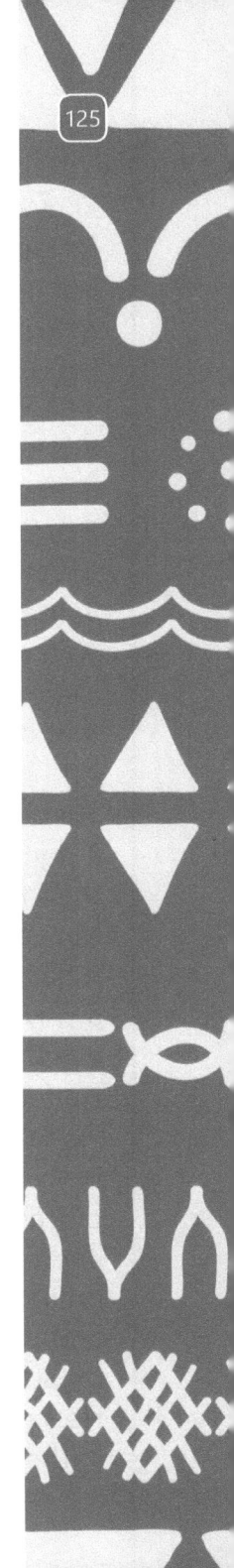

They called him Blackmaan-khulli,
for he was East Indian,
but he had an enduring connection
to Buxton.
He was born in Annandale,
which was a predominantly Indian village,
but he grew up
in Buxton.
From sunup
to sundown,
Buxton was his town.
As a child,
there was something about the village
that called him.
And kept calling him.
There was a vibe,
a rhythm to the village,
that he always felt
but could never name.
It had a personality,
a way of being,
even.
He felt it.
He felt it
in the aromas
of fresh-baked bread
and black pudding
on Saturdays,
and the hubbub of churchgoers
on Sundays.
He saw it
in the faces of the friends

BLACKA

that he made,
and he heard it
in the joy
of the voices
in the games
that they played.
And he always wondered
if "realaro," de facto Buxtonians
felt it,
for they were it.
They were its heartbeat.
And you don't feel your heartbeat
unless something
is out of whack,
like when you're having
a heart attack.
Sort of like
the way a fish
is not aware of water
until it is outside of it.
But he felt it.
He felt the throbbing
of its heartbeat
when the streets
were empty
late at night.
Its presence was always there
in the stillness.

And so, yes,
he roamed the village
day or night,

drunk or sober,
without any bother,
for all knew him.
Every man, every woman,
and every pickney
knew Blackmaan-khulli,
for he was
Blackmaan-khulli.
For he was Buxtonian,
the way Clevie, Chandaban, or Roopchand
was Buxtonian.
And even in times of discord,
of confusion,
and of tension
between blacks and Indians,
like during every election,
he still showed up
in Buxton.
And he always carried himself
like he belonged,
for he belonged.

It was during
one of those post-election periods,
those periods
of unease and distrust
and sometimes even violence,
that he visited Blacka.
He liked the peace
and the quiet
of playing chess
and disengaging

from the election confusion.
And it was during that fateful visit
that the earth shifted,
that everything changed,
that the seeds
were sown
that would forever change
the sociology
and the polity
in Guyana.
It was that day,
you see,
that birthed the BMC.

Two significant things
happened that day.
Blackmaan-khulli finally won
a game of chess against Blacka,
after almost a year
of trying.
After months
of probing, of scheming,
and of prying.
And it was a great game.
And it felt good.
Reeaaally good!
And it was after that game,
and in that mood
of euphoria
and self-accomplishment,
that he raised the issue
of Guyana's political situation

and asked
for Blacka's view.

And Blacka said:
"There is a form of insanity
in which the subject
keeps repeating the same action
almost ritualistically,
all the while expecting
at some point
a different result.
"That insanity," he said,
"has been our politics
and continues
to be our politics.
The winner-take-all,
blackmaan/khulli free-for-all
serves none,
in both the short
and the long run.
And we as a collective
have the responsibility
and need to summon the courage
and the common sense
to change it,
to sponsor a new outcome,
to unravel a conundrum
that really isn't one.
To render garbage
that which is not working.
Our government,
you see,

BLACKA

seeks to solve a problem
while being its source,
or at least
a major contributor
to its perpetuation.
And hence,
solving the problem
renders our system of government irrelevant.
That, therefore,
is the crux of the issue,
for no system
fashions its own demise.
Ultimately,
how can you achieve unity
when the reality of your politics
is disunity?
We are at that place,
I believe,
that calls for a collective
to assert its humanity,
to be
what it was meant to be,
a family.
What we live
is frankly unhealthy,
for humans were supposed
to have the intelligence
and the empathy
to support,
to love,
and to honor each other,
for we

are each other.
The fundamental problem here
is consciousness,
constipation of consciousness.
By now
the fallacy of race
should be obvious to all,
but our consciousness,
our thinking,
is still small
and rudimentary.
If we come
from the same place
and return to that same place,
if our source
is one and the same,
if we are all fragments
of that one entity,
call it what you will,
then what is the relevance
of our enmity
and distrust?
Ignorance is the perennial dust
in our collective eye.
Why?

"Our national motto
of one people,
one nation,
and one destiny
is a national joke,
and a bad one at that.

BLACKA

And if that is our aspiration,
if our ideal is union,
then our politics
didn't get the memo.
We are clearly not one people
and have never been,
and we cannot be one nation
when disunity
is our foundation.
Our destinies therefore
can never meet,
can never be one,
for when all is said
and done,
our interests remain myopic and tribal
and never panoramic
and national.

"Outside of cricket,
our society and culture
is one of separation,
of subtraction and division.
We have yet to learn the math
of addition
and multiplication,
the alchemy of union.
And in this environment
where we cannot see each other
in each other,
where we do not trust
the other,
shared governance

is the most practical interim solution
to this confusion,
in my view.
For perception
is reality.
It has always been that way.
And so
if half of the electorate
on either side
of the divide
feels underappreciated,
discriminated against,
or ignored,
whether real or imagined,
it is real.
For what you believe
is always real
for you.
There are those,
no doubt,
who would call it blasphemy,
for how could such a dispensation
be democracy?
My answer would be,
if it serves the people,
what's the tragedy?
Who cares
what the definitions
or models of others are
if they don't power your car?"

BLACKA

Then Blacka looked up.
And he looked Blackmaan-khulli
dead in the eye,
and he said:
"All that you have lived,
your entire life experience,
has brought you to this.
You may believe
that your asking of the question
that started this diatribe
is by chance
or coincidence
or even an accident.
There are no such things.
Those are words
created by people with no understanding
of the inner workings
of things.
You were being prepared
for this moment.
This is your moment.
I think
that you should start a movement.
A movement
that guarantees a government
that unifies all,
that is a call
to all
that is good and noble
in us,
which is love.
You have all the tools.

You are uniquely qualified.
You have a perspective
that is uniquely
and truly
Blackmaan-khulli.
You can see the angst
and frustrations on both sides,
but from that position
you can also see the possibilities.
You embody,
you see,
what this country seeks to be,
blackmaan/khulli,
equal parts
of a whole.
So be bold,
for you
are a hybrid soul.
If not you,
who?
If not now,
when?
You can call this movement BMC,
for Black Maan-Coolie,
but I suspect that that will offend
many a sensibility.
So tell them it means
'Betta Mus Come.'
So go forth,
for great things await you.
You are a chess player
and a great one at that,

BLACKA

as your win today demonstrated.
The politicians in this country—
a few play checkers,
but dih ress ah dem
playin litty."

GLOSSARY

"Blacka"
Vex/bex: angry.
Rubba dinky: rubber shoes.
Blow pickney: a child whose legal father is not his biological parent.
Nars: angry and violent people.
Gyaafin: talking.
Kanwa: multicolored and garish.
Backdam: backlands.
Daag: dog.
Ohmigaad: oh my god (omg).
Hignarant: angry, sullen, violent.

"Bullfrog"
Rank mook: inexperienced, wet around the ears.
Bellyache and budshit: woody shrubs.
Jumbie lash: stealth assault with a blunt instrument such as a piece of wood, usually at night.

"Stray Daag"
Obeah maan: shaman.
"He had "he fuss fat eye an feel heah",
he "fuss kamaniss an kiss heah......................
wid Snake a Hole, Fiend, Fish, Jumbie, an Took.
Translation: He had his first childhood "sexual" experiences here. He learned to gamble, swim, and trap birds, and he stole the occasional chicken and duck to cook with friends.

"First Lady"
Baad hooman: lewd woman.
Harry Wills: high wine.

"Bitta Pill"
Goadee: inguinal hernia or hydrocele.
Blow: infidelity.
"Dem gee am wan name": They gave him a nickname.

"Blackmaan-Khulli"
Jhandi: Hindu ceremony of thanksgiving that is practiced by East Indians in Guyana.
Dig Dutty: Hindu ceremony that is performed two days before a wedding in which Mother Earth is honored.
Queh-Queh: celebration of drumming, dancing, and singing in African descendant villages the night before a wedding.
Nancy: event that celebrates the life of someone in African descendant villages after they die. It is part of the "wake" tradition and is characterized by drumming and the telling of funny stories about the person who died.

Litty or jacks: childhood game played by girls with a rubber ball and knucklebones or pebbles.

ABOUT THE AUTHOR

Owen Ifill is an internal medicine and addiction medicine physician who hails from Buxton, Guyana. He has three previous publications that all explore universal and existential themes. Ifill resides with his wife and daughter in New York.

www.ingramcontent.com/pod-product-compliance
Lightning Source LLC
LaVergne TN
LVHW042251070526
838201LV00105B/299/J